Hubert Airy

AF300748

Dr. Airy's report to the local government board on an outbreak of enteric fever in Chichester

Antigonos

Hubert Airy

Dr. Airy's report to the local government board on an outbreak of enteric fever in Chichester

Reprint of the original, first published in 1879.

1st Edition 2024 | ISBN: 978-3-38676-171-0

Antigonos Verlag is an imprint of Outlook Verlagsgesellschaft mbH.

Verlag (Publisher): Outlook Verlag GmbH, Zeilweg 44, 60439 Frankfurt, Deutschland
Vertretungsberechtigt (Authorized to represent): E. Roepke, Zeilweg 44, 60439 Frankfurt, Deutschland
Druck (Print): Libri Plureos GmbH, Friedensallee 273, 22763 Hamburg, Deutschland

Dr. Airy's Report to the Local Government Board on an Outbreak of Enteric Fever in Chichester.

Edward C. Seaton, M.D.,
Medical Department,
July 24, 1879.

In consequence of a communication received from one of the inhabitants of Chichester affirming the existence there of a very grave outbreak of typhoid fever, I was directed by the Board to proceed to Chichester and inquire into the matter. This I did in April 1879.

For valuable assistance most courteously rendered to me my best thanks are due to the Mayor and all the officers of the Sanitary Authority, and other gentlemen with whom my inquiries brought me into communication. I am particularly indebted to F. J. Freeland, Esq., Medical Officer of Health, for his cordial co-operation.

On conferring with the Medical Officer of Health and several of the principal medical practitioners in the city I learnt that many of the cases of fever which had occurred up to that time had been of a somewhat uncertain type, and that considerable difference of opinion existed as to the real nature of the disease. On the one hand, there had been some cases of undoubted scarlatina, on the other there had been cases that were certainly enteric fever, but not a few had shown a mixed character, at first having the semblance of scarlatina but subsequently putting on a typhoid appearance. Many cases had presented a kind of abortive type, starting rather suddenly with rapid pulse and high temperature, as though about to prove severe, and then subsiding in five or six days without running a full course. This variety is by some practitioners recognised as characteristic of the locality, and is spoken of as " Chichester fever." Those cases which were still in progress at the time of my visit, and which I was able to examine, appeared to be of a typhoid character, though by no means well marked. Only a few of them showed any spots on the body, and in those cases the spots were scarcely more than points. Diarrhœa was by no means constantly present, though in some cases it was well pronounced. I did not hear of hæmorrhage from the bowels having occurred in any instance. The persons attacked were for the most part in delicate health previously.

My inquiries had regard more especially to a group of cases which occurred principally in the western part of the city in the month of February 1879, and which gave immediate occasion to the complaint addressed to the Local Government Board. Commencing about the 9th of February and extending through March into April, there were some 50 persons attacked, six of them fatally, in 30 houses. With regard to many of these cases I found it impossible to determine the date of attack with any precision, as they had been treated in connexion with the Infirmary, and no record of the dates of attendance had been kept. The first case of the group now spoken of occurred in the person of a student aged 25 who was attending the Theological College attached to the Cathedral. He resided in lodgings at a well-built, well-furnished house in Westgate (between L⁶ and W in annexed plan), supplied with water by the Chichester Waterworks Company, and having watercloset communicating with a cesspool at the back of the house. The basement floor was flooded more than a foot deep at the time. He is said to have been of delicate constitution and abstemious habits, drinking chiefly milk. He at first appeared to be suffering only from cold and sore throat, and was first attended on February 9th, but in a few days the disease was pronounced to be typhoid fever, and he died on the 22nd. In the same house, on February 13th, not more than four days after the date of the first attack, another student was taken ill under similar conditions. On the same day (February 13th) a child of two years was attended for typhoid fever in an

Circum-
stances of
outbreak.

adjoining street (Orchard Street, O in plan). Here water was obtained from a private well used by two families in common. At the back of the house there is a slop-drain, communicating with an arched watercourse which runs under the street. At the end of a small back-garden is a privy over a cesspit, which has not been emptied for two years.

Two days later (February 15th) two other families in Westgate living close to the house where the first cases occurred, supplied with water from the water-works, and having separate privies and cesspools, were invaded by the same disease, two children in each family being attacked. In one of these families there were four children, and it was noticed that the two who were attacked were the two who drank milk.

Three days later (February 18th) typhoid fever broke out in a family of the upper class residing in Canon Lane (c.l. in plan), in quite a different part of the city from Westgate or Orchard Street. The students who resided in West-gate had, it is true, frequently visited Canon Lane up to the time when they were taken ill, but this personal communication does not appear to have been of a nature likely to spread typhoid fever. Subsequently another family in Canon Lane that had previously had several members sick with scarlatina was, in addition, attacked by typhoid. Both these families had water from the waterworks and drainage into separate cesspools, and both had milk from the same dairy.

And now it was noticed that not only these two families but all the families in which the above-mentioned cases occurred were supplied with milk from a particular dairy in Orchard Street. In the subsequent spread of the disease also a similar coincidence was generally, if not universally, observed.

These facts were enough to raise a suspicion that the milk of the dairy in question was the vehicle of typhoid infection.

Before adopting such a conclusion it will be necessary to consider other possible modes of conveyance of this disease, and see that they are excluded in the case before us.

Water may be briefly dismissed, for, of the 30 houses infected, 17 had wells and 13 were supplied by the Chichester Waterworks Company, and we cannot suppose these independent sources to have been simultaneously poisoned.

In respect of drainage there was indeed an apparent community of unwholesome conditions among the greater number of the houses infected, those, namely, in Orchard Street and the adjoining part of Westgate, which will claim further notice below; but these conditions did not affect Canon Lane, which shared in the outbreak.

In making inquiries concerning the supply of milk from the Orchard Street dairy I found every disposition on the part of the owner to assist me, and I am satisfied that no information of any importance to the inquiry was withheld.

The Medical Officer of Health had been furnished with a list of all the families which at the time of the outbreak were directly supplied with milk from the Orchard Street dairy. They numbered 53. To these should be added about six that obtained milk indirectly or in very small quantities from the same source, making a total of 59. Of these about 26, or 43 per cent., had, in the course of the epidemic, more or less distinct cases of typhoid fever. In the same locality in which the Orchard Street milk was chiefly distributed, namely, Orchard Street, Westgate, West Street, and Canon Lane, there were about 40 families supplied by other dairymen, nine of them being also part customers of the Orchard Street dairy. Among these families, as far as I could learn, there had been no case of typhoid fever (excluding one or two doubtful cases described as " febricula "), except in five of the nine families that also took part of their supply from Orchard Street. These facts, viewed by the light of previous experience as to the distribution of fever along with milk, appeared to show a high probability that the milk from the Orchard Street dairy was the chief, if not the sole, factor involved in the distribution of typhoid fever ; but there was one fact which still required explanation. In Tower Street (T in plan) which lies nearer the centre of the city than the region principally affected, the Orchard Street dairy served seven families, and among these seven there was no case of fever. This might have been a mere chance, (for we know that some persons habitually escape, where a number have appeared to be equally exposed to conditions productive of this fever,) but on inquiry of the milkman I learnt that Tower Street was the last street he served in his daily round, and that it happened more often than not that by the time he came to Tower Street his own supply had run out, and he was obliged to purchase a quart or two from another dairyman to complete the amount required. Thus it appears that there was a difference between the supply to Tower Street and that to other parts of the same milk-walk. (It should be mentioned, however, that a child in one of the Tower Street families was invariably supplied with milk from one particular cow belonging to the Orchard Street dairy.) These facts regarding Tower Street are perhaps not very important, but as far as they go they support the conclusion above indicated.

Visiting the dairy in Orchard Street (D in plan), I was shown the place where the milkcans were washed, in a sort of back-kitchen. The water is drawn by pump from a well under the same roof. It looks clear and bright, and is preferred by the neighbours to most of the well-water in the same street. It cannot, however, be considered safe from pollution, seeing that there is a privy-pit only 8 yards from the well in one direction, and a slop-cesspool 9 yards off in the other. The pump drippings run in an open brick channel to a small catch-pit close outside the back kitchen wall, and thence in a covered drain to the cesspool. The well is situated within a sharp bend of the watercourse which I have mentioned as underlying Orchard Street, and it is conceivable that it might derive impure admixture from that watercourse on one side or the other. The nature of the soil, which is gravel overlying London clay, gives facility for soakage from the cesspools into the wells.

Samples of this water have been analysed by Dr. A. Dupré of the Westminster Hospital. The analysis is subjoined to this Report, Dr. Dupré concludes: "If the well is deep, and there are no sources of contamination " *near*, I should pronounce the water as a fairly pure chalk water. If, " however, there are any sources of contamination near, I think it is highly " probable that the water is slightly contaminated by sewage or urine which " have not passed through any great thickness of earth, as otherwise more " nitric acid would be found." The proximity of the above-mentioned privy, &c. favour the latter view.

There was no history of typhoid fever having occurred in this house or anywhere close by it previous to the outbreak in February, and in the absence of such history we have no right to assume that the well-water was specifically contaminated.

From the dairy I went with the milkman to the meadows (M) where his five cows were pasturing. These meadows lie immediately to the south-west of the city, on either side of the stream, the " Lavant," which, when flowing, (for it is dry in the summer and autumn,) washes the eastern, southern, and western outskirts of the city, receiving in its course large quantities of filth, and finally makes its way in a south-westerly direction through these meadows to the sea (Chichester Harbour) at Appledram. The cows no doubt drink of this stream when it is flowing; when it is dry they find water at a spring in the meadow. The cows themselves have ailed nothing. The operation of milking is performed in an old boarded five-stalled milking-hovel (H) which stands in the meadow about 35 yards from the Lavant stream. The milkman, having brought the cans clean from the dairy, takes them straight to the hovel, never rinsing them in the stream. Having gathered his cows, and girded himself with a coarse apron, he proceeds to wash the udder of the cow he is about to milk, the udder being often soiled with the cow's own droppings or from lying in the meadow. For this purpose he resorts to a bucket which has been filled from the Lavant stream, when running. In times of drought he carries with him some water from the dairy pump instead. Having cleansed the udder and his own hands he rapidly wipes them with his apron, and proceeds with his milking. His hands occasionally are moistened with the milk, and anything remaining from the previous washing on his hands or the cow's teats is thus brought into contact with the milk. In this way an extremely minute portion of Lavant water may become mixed with the milk in the can. I was quite satisfied that there had been no wilful dilution of the milk, either with

Lavant water or pump water, not only because of the manifest honesty of the milkman, but from the general accordance of testimony among his customers as to the richness of the milk. I heard also that an analysis of the milk had been made, and gave no evidence of any dilution.

The cows were milked twice a day; in the morning the filled cans stood awhile at the dairy; in the afternoon the milk was delivered on the way back from the hovel.

The act of milking, then, is the only moment at which I can detect any opportunity for specific contamination of the milk. (It will appear below that the Lavant water probably contained the poison of enteric fever.) Whether so minute a quantity of the poison could so rapidly impart its poisonous properties to the milk as to cause enteric fever in so large a proportion of those who drank of it, is a question which I must leave open. We have some reason to think that very small quantities of infective material can go on multiplying when introduced into milk, somewhat as they go on multiplying when they produce disease in the human body, and it may be suggested as conceivable that the warmth of the milker's hands and of the fresh-drawn milk might accelerate such multiplication.

That the Lavant stream at the end of January and beginning of February was carrying typhoid excreta, there can, I think, be little room for doubt. Where the Lavant first approaches the city coming from the chalk downs beyond Goodwood, it runs alongside the high road which leads to Arundel; and diverging slightly from the road it leaves room (at L^1) for a row of cottages of the poorest class to fill the space between, with back-yards about three paces deep, abutting immediately upon the Lavant. The privies stand on either side of the stream, most of them at the very edge, those across the stream being accessible by a plank-bridge. The insecure brickwork of the privy pits allows excremental matter to ooze visibly into the bed of the stream. The inhabitants of these cottages were supposed to draw their drinking water from wells sunk in their narrow back-yards, but one at least of these wells yielded water of such bad quality that one of the families it was intended to serve resorted confessedly to the Lavant, when running, in preference to the well. Slops were sometimes poured into the privies, but more frequently into the Lavant course. I saw a child deal thus with the contents of two chamber-vessels evidently as a matter of habit. Among these cottages there was a good deal of typhoid fever in the fourth quarter of 1878, extending into January of the present year. One practitioner alone attended 23 cases in only six families, the majority of them being young children. The type of disease was not severe. There was no fatal case. In most of them there was absence of diarrhœa; and only two or three of them showed a characteristic eruption.

The first case was that of a girl of 14 who was taken ill about a week after returning from hop-picking in the east of Hampshire. The exact date of her return could not be remembered with certainty, but the interval between the return and the attack was probably less than the usual incubation-period of typhoid fever. I have made inquiry of the Medical Officer of Health for the district in which this girl had been employed at hop-harvest (Arthur Curtis, Esq., of Alton), and learn from him that there were in August cases of typhoid fever in Selborne, the next parish to that in which the girl had worked. Nothing of importance, however, can be ascertained as to her opportunities of contracting fever while away from home.

It cannot be doubted that in the last quarter of 1878 the Lavant course at the east end of the city received, in one way or another, a quantity of excrementitious matter from these persons in St. Pancras (the name of this quarter of the city) who were suffering from typhoid fever. The Lavant at the time was dry. How soon it began to flow again I failed to ascertain; but it appears to have been later than usual, probably not before the severe frost set in. The rainfall of the quarter was a little below the average. The winter was exceptionally severe; and it appears probable that there was no free flow of water in the Lavant until the latter part of January. The rainfall for that month, as recorded at the Chichester Infirmary, was 5·42 inches. The average annual rainfall at Chichester, deduced from ten years' record, kindly communicated to me by Dr. Tyacke of Chichester, is about 29 inches. It would seem, therefore, that the rainfall in January was more than twice as great as the monthly average; and we may be sure that by the end of the month the stream was running in full volume.

After washing the privies of St. Pancras, the Lavant skirts the south-eastern corner of the city walls (L²) sometimes in culvert under houses and sometimes open, passes in culvert under South Street, and is then divided (at L³), a cut having been made in modern times which (unless closed by a penstock) takes the main body of the water southward to join the original channel lower down. The old channel continues to skirt the city walls in a westerly direction. At the south-west corner of the walls the stream is again sub-divided (at L⁴), another modern cut taking the bulk of the water westward, while the old channel entering a culvert turns due north, and passes under a long garden, under Westgate, and under the whole range of houses on the east side of Orchard Street, still following the contour of the city walls until they begin to trend in a north-easterly direction. At this point (L⁵) the old channel leaves the wall, takes a sharp turn round to the west, emerging for a few yards into daylight, and returns in a south-westerly direction again in culvert past a large brewery, under Westgate (at L⁶), under a large tannery, and then out southwards into the daylight and the meadows (M), where it joins the modern cut No. 2 (at L⁷), and cut No. 1 (at L⁸), and then is carried under the railway and proceeds seaward. These (M) are the meadows in which the cows of the Orchard Street dairy were pastured and milked; and it was at this point that water was drawn from the Lavant, to be used for cleansing purposes in the milking hovel.

The stream in these meadows contains not only a portion of the filth it has received in St. Pancras, but also whatever tribute of impurity it may gather in St. Bartholomew, outside the western walls; and I heard in Orchard Street, where the stream is in culvert, of night-men who, to facilitate their work, had taken bricks out of the arch of the culvert and shot their unsavoury charge wholesale into the Lavant course. Moreover, almost every house in Orchard Street has a slop-drain giving into the same convenient sewer, which also receives the surface drainage of West Street and Westgate, and, by a tributary sewer (c.d.) the surface and slop-drainage of the northern parts of the city both within and without the walls. The brewery and tannery above mentioned add largely to the pollution of the stream.

The southern and western reaches of the Lavant have very little fall: the former (L³ to L⁴) only 8 inches in 1,250 feet; the latter (L⁴ to L⁵) only 6 inches in 1,200 feet.* Indeed in the latter, at its southern end where it enters the culvert under Dr. Tyacke's garden (at L⁴), I more often saw the water coming out than going in. At the same time, curiously enough, a strong outflow was maintained at the north end (L⁵), proving that somewhere in its underground course the steam received a large accession, probably from springs at the foot of the gravel bank on which the city stands. Nothing, however, was known of any such springs by men who had passed through the whole length of this culvert. The fact was established beyond doubt by means of an experiment which the City Surveyor, Mr. J. Kerwood, made at my request. He temporarily dammed the old channel in its southern reach (just west of L³), turning the whole stream along the modern cut No. 1 (L³ to R), so that it was quite certain that nothing entered the culvert under Dr. Tyacke's garden (at L⁴). The dam was maintained for the greater part of a day, and during the whole of that time a copious stream continued to flow out with undiminished volume at the north end of Orchard Street (L⁵). It was remarked by one

---

* The modern cuts which I have spoken of give the water a much more rapid fall. The old channel does not follow the most naturally advantageous direction; and its course if natural can only be explained on the supposition that the stream has meandered. But a meandering stream will be found as a rule to have its convexities scouring at the foot of the higher ground, while in its concavities it has the lower and gently-shelving shore which it is gradually relinquishing as it eats further into the " scour " on the opposite side. Now these reaches of the Lavant show no such feature: on the contrary, in their general concavity they contain the gentle hill of gravel on which the walled city stands, and all around they have the soft meadow soil which in the days when rivers had their own way would certainly have yielded at every convexity of the stream. It seems not improbable that the Lavant may have had originally a more direct course, and may have been artficially diverted in order to aid in the defensive works of the city. If this be so, the diversion must have been effected at an early date, for in a map of the 17th century the river is shown as having the same circuitous course as at present, but entirely open throughout. A map dated 1812, shows the river still open except outside Eastgate, Southgate, and Westgate, and under part of Orchard Street.

of the inhabitants, who draws water from this stream for garden purposes, that in most years it continues to flow at this end for some time after the southern reach is dry.

From what I saw at the entrance to the culvert under Dr. Tyacke's garden, it was quite evident that the water it contained, at least in its southern portion, was virtually stagnant, except at times when the Lavant was unusually high. The culvert is 5 or 6 feet wide, and about 4 feet high to the crown of the arch. The bottom is not bricked, and is very irregular in its bed. Much deposit is believed to have accumulated. Remembering the pollution of the stream in the upper part of its course. and also what it must receive from the street gutters and slop drains in Westgate and Orchard Street, we may be quite sure that this great sewer contains a large body of stagnant filth. Except at its two ends, which are open, this sewer is unprovided with means of ventilation in its whole length of 1,200 feet. When the wind sets against one end of it, a characteristic sewer smell proceeds from the other.

The Orchard Street slop-drains give direct into this tunnel, and previous to the recent outbreak of fever, these drains were trapped imperfectly, or not at all, and foul smells were sometimes perceived from them. Bearing in mind the specific pollution of the Lavant stream from the previous outbreak of typhoid fever in St. Pancras, it would appear quite possible that typhoid fever, subsequently breaking out in Westgate and Orchard Street, might be due to the escape of poisonous air from the covered branch of the Lavant, through the defective traps; and I certainly would not venture to say that no case has arisen from this cause; but the facts relating to special incidence of fever on customers of a particular dairy are such as could not be explained on the hypothesis that the outbreak as a whole was due to sewer-air or any other cause than infected milk. Whether I have been able to point out the actual *mode* in which the milk became infected, is a point which, I feel, may very well be questioned.

It remains to notice certain features in the sanitary condition of the city, which, though not intimately involved in the preceding inquiry, have an important general bearing upon the health of the inhabitants.

The sanitary condition of Chichester was the subject of an inquiry by Dr. Seaton for the Privy Council in 1865. I may perhaps be allowed to refer to Dr. Seaton's Report, and point out in what respects the condition of the city has been improved in the 14 years that have passed since he made his inspection.

During the seven years, 1858-64, the average annual number of deaths was 196, and the average annual death-rate Dr. Seaton calculated, after all allowances, not less than 22 per 1,000. In the past 14 years, 1865-78, the yearly average of deaths was 178·7. From this number a deduction should be made in calculating the local death-rate, on account of deaths of patients brought into the Infirmary from other places than Chichester. If we reduce the average yearly mortality to 170, and take the population as given at the census of 1871, viz., 8,205, the average annual death-rate per 1,000 comes to 20·7. This indicates a certain improvement in the last 14 years; but the death-rate is still much higher than it ought to be in a place possessing the natural advantages of Chichester.

Dr. Seaton pointed out that deaths from fever had been very frequent in the period under his review, averaging in five years as many as 13 per annum. In the past nine years, 1870-8, the annual average of deaths from fever has been 5·4 or 0·66 per 1,000 inhabitants, and the highest number in any one year has been 10. Diarrhœa in the same period has caused on an average five deaths yearly. The prevalence of enteric fever among children which was noticed by Dr. Seaton still continues, as exemplified in the outbreak of last autumn in St. Pancras.

Diphtheria causes an average of two deaths every year.

In regard to drainage, the city is in the same state now as it was 14 years ago. I have already described how the Lavant course receives the drainage of the houses that are built beside or over it. This serves as the main sewer for the outskirts of the city. There is a smaller one at the back of Orchard Terrace, outside the north walls, which for a length of about 150 yards appears as an open ditch, known as the " Campus " ditch (c. d. in plan) and

Sanitary condition of Chichester.

Mortality.

Drainage.

finally joins the Lavant at its bend at the top of Orchard Street (at L⁵). But
the great bulk of the city is still drained into cesspools, sometimes separate
from, sometimes identical with, the privy pits, and often in dangerously
close relation with wells, from which a large proportion of the drinking water
is still obtained.

Dr. Seaton recommended that steps should be taken for establishing a complete system of drainage. A few months later in the same year (1865) the
Town Council consulted Mr. Lawson, C.E., F.G.S., who prepared a plan of
sewerage and water works. The proposed sewerage works he estimated at
12,500*l.* His plan was to drain the city entirely by gravitation, and dispose
of the sewage by irrigation on 90 acres of land near the outfall of the Lavant
into Chichester Harbour, at Appledram, about a mile and a quarter from the
city. Looking at the proposal without technical engineering knowledge, I am
struck by the small irrigation slope which the plan would provide, if the
cellars are to be duly drained, and any land except what is already swampy
to be irrigated.

The Town Council took no action on Mr. Lawson's report.

In the following year Mr. Arnold Taylor, of the Local Government Act
Office, held an inquiry at Chichester under the 49th section of the Sanitary
Act, 1866, in consequence of a memorial forwarded by Dr. Swainson, of
Chichester, complaining of the unwholesome state of the city. Mr. Taylor's
report entirely endorsed Dr. Seaton's description, and his final recommenda-
tions with regard to the drainage question were to the effect that the Town
Council, if not prepared to adopt Mr. Lawson's plan, should consult some
other competent engineer.

Accordingly in the following year (1867), Mr. Hawksley, C.E., was called
in to advise the Town Council on the suggested system of drainage, &c. In
his report he took occasion to express his " decided conviction and conclusion
" that Chichester has been unjustifiably charged with being an unhealthy
and unclean city," and supported his conclusion by an appeal to the mortality
of the city in the twelve years 1856–67, averaging 198 deaths per annum,
in a stationary population of 8,045, a death-rate of 24·6 per 1,000. " Having
" satisfactorily ascertained, though from limited data, that Chichester is not
" an unhealthy city," Mr. Hawksley proceeds to give his opinion that " the
" internal drainage of the city may be postponed, at all events for some
" years, if a competent supply of water be promptly introduced." He adds,
however, a word of cautious warning, " that the city will continue to be open
" to mistrust and imputation, grounded or groundless, until some system of
" internal drainage be adopted." This contingency the Town Council have
accepted, and Chichester remains undrained.

The state of the Lavant course has been examined, at the instance of the
Town Council, by both the above-named engineers, and also, in 1873, by
Mr. J. E. Greatorex, C.E., but not so much in regard to its abuse for drainage
purposes as with a view of preventing the floods to which it is liable in its
upper course. Mr. Lawson and Mr. Hawksley both recommended that the
channel should be widened and straightened, and that its fall should be
improved by lowering its bed at the south end of Dr. Tyacke's garden. The
effect of this would be that the whole stream (except the overflow by cut
No. 1 (L³ to R) would pass along cut No. 2 (L⁴ to L⁷), and no part of it would
enter the culvert under Dr. Tyacke's garden. That branch (L⁴ to L⁵) would
thus become more stagnant and, if still used as a sewer, more offensive than
ever.

Mr. Greatorex agrees in recommending a straightening and lowering of the
main channel, and says, with regard to the Orchard Street branch, " It being
" evident that the portion of this course from Westgate to the north end of
" Orchard Street acts as the drain or sewer for the premises in that street ;
" under such circumstances it cannot be abolished ; and it also receives the
" storm-water of Westgate and other localities ; and the only means of cleansing
" it would be to construct a penstock on the main course at the south entrance,
" holding the water back and turning it through that channel, so periodically
" flushing it out. This step, however, perhaps could only be effected at the
" risk of flooding the basements of houses higher up the stream."

This objection appears fatal to the scheme of flushing what would be a
high-level sewer from what would be a low-level stream.

It is evident from the experiment made for me by Mr. Kerwood, that this arched branch of the Lavant course plays an important part in draining the subsoil, and it requires to be thoroughly explored at a time when no water is entering it from the south, with a view to determine the point or points at which the spring water enters it.

The flooding of the Lavant in St. Pancras concerns the health as well as the comfort of the inhabitants, and requires to be kept in view by the Sanitary Authority. In order to diminish the risk of floods a relief-pipe has been laid from between Eastgate and Southgate to a canal basin south of the railway, (from L^2 to c.b.), but it is doubtful whether this overflow pipe is large enough to be of much service, and it would probably be found useful to enlarge it.

Water.

To speak now of water supply :—

The city is full of wells, and full of cesspools, and the porous, gravelly nature of the soil gives every facility for the soakage of filth from the cesspools into the wells. It is notorious that this often happens ; much of the well water is wholly unusable. I saw a portion of the leaden suction-pipe of a pump that had been taken down ; it was coated internally with a thick black deposit. On the other hand, many of the wells are in good repute for the quality of the water they yield. In sinking a new well care is taken, as far as possible, to avoid the neighbourhood of existing cesspools, but new cesspools are planted without equal regard to the interests of the neighbouring wells.

At the time of Dr. Seaton's inspection the danger arising from pollution of the wells was one which affected the whole population of the city, inasmuch as there was no other source but the wells from which drinking water could be obtained ; but this danger is not so universal now, for within the last four years water works have been established by a private company, who at the present time supply 250 houses out of a total of about 1,600. They have tapped a strong spring at the head of Fishbourne Creek, a mile and a half to the west of Chichester, at the junction of the plastic clay formation with the chalk ; in sinking the well the water rose in such volume that they were unable to go deeper than 27 feet, and even at that depth some of the workmen's tools had to be left at the bottom. The water has been analysed by Dr. J. Muter, F.C.S., (March 10th, 1879), and pronounced to be " a water of very excellent quality indeed." It is somewhat hard (20 degrees of Clarke's scale), but the hardness is reduced to four degrees by boiling. There appears no reason to apprehend any pollution of this water at its source. The well is enclosed in the pumping station with the duplicate engines, either of which will throw 10,000 gallons an hour. The level of the water in the well is reduced by 14 feet when the engine is working, and is restored in twenty minutes after stopping the engine, the water overflowing in a strong stream into the creek. The mains are carried direct into the city, supplying consumers on the way. At the Market Cross in the centre of the city the principal main turns north, and is carried up the London Road to a reservoir (w.r.) opposite the barracks, at a height of about 50 feet above the highest point of the city. A smaller tank is raised another 50 feet on a tower beside the reservoir, for the supply of consumers on the neighbouring high ground and for additional pressure on the city mains in case of fire in the cathedral. The service is constant, during the night by gravitation, and during the day by engine power overcoming gravitation. The supply is ample for the whole population. It only needs that greater alacrity should be shown by the citizens in availing themselves of this valuable boon, and by the Sanitary Authority in enforcing the disuse of polluted wells.

Nuisances removal.

Dr. Seaton reported that the Nuisances Removal Acts were very inefficiently administered. There has been considerable improvement since then, but it cannot be said that the powers conferred by the Public Health Act, 1875, upon the Town Council as Urban Sanitary Authority have as yet been fully exercised in this respect. There is still much delay in procuring the removal of refuse accumulations. A contractor agrees to do it, who is supposed to be under the supervision of the city surveyor, but is practically allowed his own way. He makes a depôt of refuse (d.r. on map) close to a public road, outside the north-east corner of the city.

The emptying of privies is left to private management. I met with instances where the privy pit had not been emptied for eight years.

The great nuisance which Dr. Seaton found existing in connection with the fortnightly cattle market held in the streets of the city has been entirely removed by the formation, in 1869, of a new cattle market (c.m.) outside the south-eastern walls. The expense of this important work was 15,000*l.* Cattle market.

Under the Public Health Act, 1872, the Town Council appointed one and the same person as medical officer of health and inspector of nuisances. The combined offices are at present held by F. J. Freeland, Esq., at a salary of 100*l.* a year. The duties of an inspector of nuisances are hardly compatible with the position and engagements of a professional man; and while fully recognising the diligence and efficiency with which those duties are performed under disadvantageous circumstances, I cannot help feeling that it would be better if an additional officer were appointed to discharge the duties of inspector of nuisances. " Administration.

The Sanitary Authority have no byelaws.

Neither have they any fit hospital for the isolation of cases of infectious disease. An old " pest house " still stands, but is wholly unequal to the requirements of the district.

In conclusion, I would point out that while considerable improvement has been made, and is still in progress, in respect of water supply, nuisance removal, and general sanitary supervision, and especially noting the complete and most satisfactory reform that has been made in the matter of the cattle market—a general improvement to which we may fairly ascribe a corresponding diminution of mortality—there yet remain grave defects in the sanitary condition of the city, which it will doubtless be the anxious desire and endeavour of the Town Council to remove as speedily as shall be consistent with their financial position.

HUBERT AIRY.

Local Government Board,
   May 1879.

Recommendations.

1. It is requisite that the Sanitary Authority should adopt and carry out some scheme of sewerage and drainage which shall convey the slops and watercloset discharges to a safe distance from the city.

   As rapidly as it becomes practicable to deal with the cesspools that are now polluting the soil of the city, such cesspools should be carefully cleaned out and filled up, and all filth removed to a safe distance.

2. By all means in their power the Sanitary Authority should endeavour to procure the alteration of privies with uncemented pits to some other form of privy or closet in which the receptacle shall be so contrived as to prevent soakage of filth into the surrounding soil. The Board's Official Report on Means of Excrement Disposal in Towns and Villages may be usefully consulted in this connexion.

   Every privy-pit so disused should be carefully cleaned out and filled up with wholesome soil, and all the filth taken from it should be removed to a safe distance.

3. With regard to the Lavant course :

   Steps should be taken to prevent the pollution of this stream (or its dry bed) by slop or privy drainage. It ought not to receive anything fouler than surface water.

   The escape of flood waters would be facilitated if the Lavant course were straightened and lowered, as unanimously recommended by every engineer who has examined the question, and if a freer overflow to the canal basin were provided.

   The covered part of the Lavant course, from the south end of Dr. Tyacke's garden to the north end of Orchard Street, requires attention to prevent nuisance arising.

4. Wells known to be polluted should be closed, and the owners should be required to have pure water laid on.

5. The Sanitary Authority should have a proper place for the isolation of cases of infectious disease.

6. The Sanitary Authority should have a code of byelaws, and with this view they would do well to consider the model byelaws issued by the Local Government Board.

7. The Medical Officer of Health should be assisted by an officer, who should take the duties proper to an inspector of nuisances.

PLAN OF CHICHESTER.

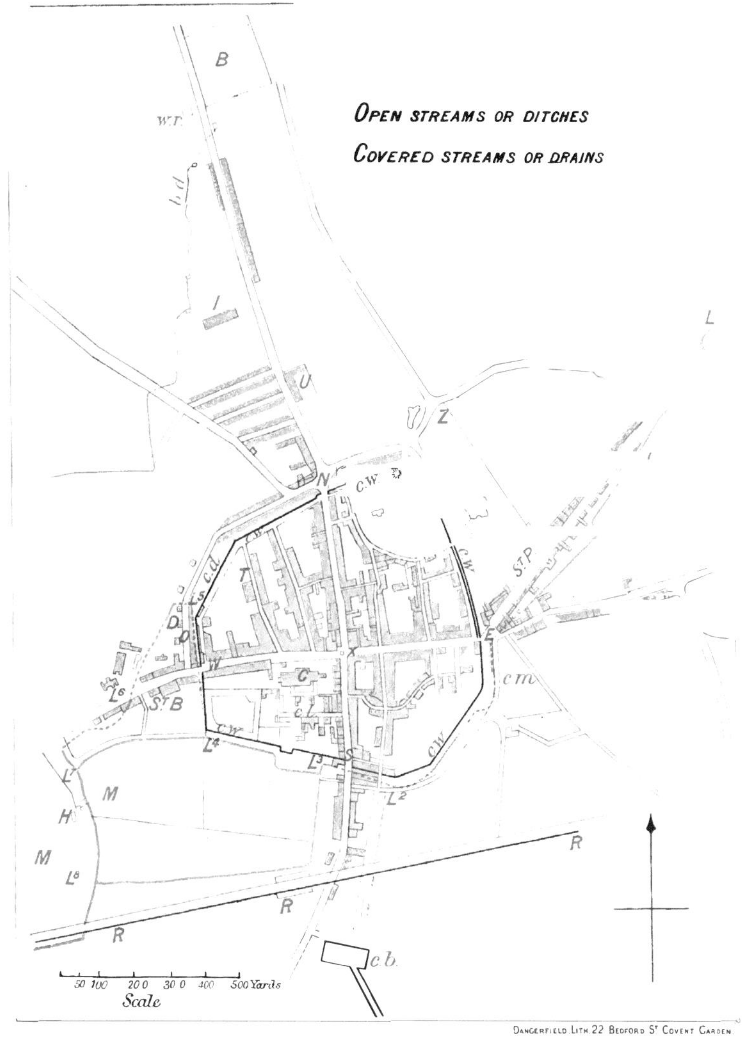

DANGERFIELD LITH. 22 BEDFORD ST COVENT GARDEN.

B Barracks	L⁴ Stream branches again: modern cut (Nº 2,) goes west.	O Orchard Street.
C Cathedral		S.T.P. St. Pancras.
D Dairy, in Orchard Street	L⁴toW Stream in Culvert under Dr Tyacke's garden.	R Railway.
E Eastgate		S Southgate.
H Milking hovel	WtoL⁵ Stream in Culvert under Orchard Street.	T Tower Street.
I Infirmary		U Union Workhouse
L Lavant Stream	L⁶ Stream in Culvert returning under Westgate.	W Westgate
L¹ Houses with enteric fever in 4th quarter of 1878.		X Market Cross.
	L⁷ Junction with cut (Nº 2.)	Z Depôt of City Refuse.
L² Inlet of flood relief pipe.	L⁸ Junction with cut (Nº 1.	b.d. Barracks drainage (overflow)
L³ Stream branches: modern cut (Nº 1.) goes south.	M Meadows	c.b. Canal basin
	N Northgate.	c.d. "Campus" ditch.

c.l. Canon Lane   c.w. City Walls.

c.m. Cattle Market   w.r. Water reservoir.

APPENDIX.

REPORT on a Sample of Water received from the Medical Department of the Local Government Board, May 9th, 1879.

Sample contained in two Winchester quart bottles, stoppered, stoppers tied over and secured by seal (F.), seal unbroken. Each bottle labelled. The one " Chichester, May 8/79, Moore's pump water, Orchard Street, No. 1 Sample "; the other, " Duplicate, May 8, Moore's pump water, Orchard Street, Chichester."

The water is clear, has a very pale greenish-yellow colour, is tasteless and inodorous; it yields no deposit on standing. It contains only a very small amount of nitric acid, yields but little albuminoid ammonia, and absorbs a small proportion of oxygen from permanganate. In these three respects the water must be pronounced as fairly pure. On the other hand, the water contains a very large amount of ammonia, rather much chlorine, and, comparatively speaking, very much phosphoric acid.

Under these circumstances it is scarcely possible to give a definite opinion on the water without having an exact knowledge of the surroundings of the pump.

If the well is deep, and there are no sources of contamination *near*, I should pronounce the water as a fairly pure chalk water. If, however, there are any sources of contamination near, I think it is highly probable that the water is slightly contaminated by sewage or urine, which have not passed through any great thickness of earth, as otherwise more nitric acid would be found.

The analytical details are given in the table annexed:—

Appearance	Clear.
Colour	- Pale greenish-yellow.
Taste	- Tasteless.
Smell	- Inodorous.
Deposit	- None.
Nitrous acid	- None.
Phosphoric acid	- Very much.
Metallic impurities	- None.
Hardness before boiling	- 22 degrees.
„ after	$3 \cdot 5$ „

Grains per Gallon.

Oxygen absorbed from permanganate	- $0 \cdot 018$
Total dry residue	- $30 \cdot 38$
Consisting of volatile matters	- $0 \cdot 70$
„ fixed salts	- $29 \cdot 68$
Chlorine	- $3 \cdot 36$
Nitric acid ($N_2 O_3$)	- $0 \cdot 161$
Ammonia	$0 \cdot 0746$
Albuminoid ammonia	- $0 \cdot 0045$

A. DUPRÉ,

Westminster Hospital,
    May 15th, 1879.

LONDON:
Printed by GEORGE E. EYRE and WILLIAM SPOTTISWOODE,
Printers to the Queen's most Excellent Majesty.
For Her Majesty's Stationery Office.
[2736.—100.—7/79.]